Qm.,

thanks
for the title

Broken

Accidents

Other works by Phlip Arima

poetry books
Damaged
Beneath the Beauty

CDs (audio)
The Inside Edge

anthologies
Voices Under the Guise of Darkness vol.3
Poetry Nation
Burning Ambitions
Written in the Skin
Shard Anthology II
Playing in the Asphalt Garden
Shard Anthology

Broken Accidents

fiction by
Phlip Arima

INSOMNIAC PRESS

Edited by Adrienne Weiss
Designed by Marijke Friesen
Back cover photo by Monica S. Kuebler

National Library of Canada Cataloguing in Publication
Data

Arima, Phlip, 1963-
Broken accidents / Phlip Arima.

ISBN 1-894663-39-X

I. Title.

PS8551.R762B76 2003   C813'.54
C2003-900708-1
PR9199.3.A536B76 2003

The Author is grateful to Quinlan Arima for the title;
and to Kyril Chen and Ed Keenan for their generous
assistance.

The publisher gratefully acknowledges the support of
the Canada Council, the Ontario Arts Council and the
Department of Canadian Heritage through the Book
Publishing Industry Development Program. We
acknowledge the support of the Government of
Ontario through the Ontario Media Development
Corporation's Ontario Book Initiative.

Printed and bound in Canada

Insomniac Press
192 Spadina Avenue, Suite 403
Toronto, Ontario, Canada, M5T 2C2
www.insomniacpress.com

THE CANADA COUNCIL | LE CONSEIL DES ARTS
FOR THE ARTS | DU CANADA
SINCE 1957 | DEPUIS 1957

ONTARIO ARTS COUNCIL
CONSEIL DES ARTS DE L'ONTARIO

For Martha and Jennifer

crashcras

(Happy Birthday)	9
My Decisions	11
Naked	15
A Better Way	19
Dead Company	25
Seizure	31
Waiting for a Friend	35
Yucky	41
Chicken Noodle Soup	49
Togetherness	57
The Music Lover	61
Intimacy	67
All the Same	69
Pickled Mango	77

Perhaps □ 12
I Am □ 47
It Seems □ 72

delevations

tatsstats

83   In the Grey

91   Trafficked

95   Blue Denim

103   Dropping Out

107   Yawn

111   Just Me

115   Wireless

119   The Importance of Sunglasses

123   Entertainment

125   Punk is Beat

129   Answers

135   The Key

139   Without a Splash

143   Had Enough

149   Thirst

Separate and Alone □ 92
Looking Within □ 113
Exiting the Elevator □ 136

delevations

Of course I remembered your birthday.
I remember everybody's birthday.
Don't take it so personally.

My Decisions

Today I put my parents down. They were old, and mother wasn't well. The medical bills were getting to be too much and I was tired of constantly driving out to visit them. Soon, home care would be necessary, another expense. Who needs it? She'd had a full life: just one husband from the age of nineteen, a nice house, a loving son.

Sure, there were things she never got to do, things she wanted to experience. We would talk about the opportunities she'd missed. I know she always dreamed of travelling to Paris, but it was a little late for that now. Even if I hadn't put her down, the logistics would've been impossible. And I don't think she'd really have enjoyed it, let alone remembered it.

There was nothing wrong with father. He was still jogging every day, watching his videos, popular down at the pub. There really wasn't anything he couldn't do. But without mother, he'd be lonely. I figured there'd be no end to his complaining. Not my idea of a good time, *thank-you-very-much*. So I had him put down too.

The staff at The Centre assured me this was best for all concerned. Their counsel really helped me keep the situation in the right perspective. There were nights when I lay awake staring up at the ceiling, unable to keep the anxiety down. I called the twenty-four hour hotline several times. They suggested I attend a Guilt Anonymous meeting, join a group. But I don't want to be around those kind

Perhaps I live in an elevator with wall-to-wall carpeting. It has a full-length mirror and fan for ventilation. It might not sound like

of people. Besides, I don't have a guilty conscience.

Father was less than thrilled by my decision. It took a lot of convincing to get him to be reasonable. I threw a big party for him the night before, spared no expense. He seemed to enjoy it, though he was pretty exhausted by the time it ended. Drunk too. But I guess that really shouldn't've surprised me. After all, it was his last night.

Luckily, because of the population crisis, I received a two-for-one discount on the injections. The new government really cares about the people. The Centre had a special room just for couples. The technician hooked mother and father to the same I.V. and talked to them throughout the entire procedure. I think her words made it a lot easier for them. Or maybe it was just her tone of voice. Either way, they seemed quite calm when she prepared the needle. She was so considerate of their feelings. And my feelings too. After she inserted the needle, she let me push the plunger down.

Mother and father held hands and looked into each other's eyes all the way

much, but it's really quite spacious. If I lie down diagonally from one corner to the other, I can actually straighten my legs. It was a

Philip Arima

13

through the entire procedure. I could tell they were still, after all these years, deeply in love. It was so romantic. It choked me up. But I didn't cry. That would've been so embarrassing.

Tomorrow they're going to be cremated. Again, I got a discount—a free urn to keep their ashes in. There were so many to choose from. I spent the entire afternoon in the showroom. I finally decided on a simple stainless steel number. I was really tempted to go for this tall brass one, but it didn't have a screw-top lid.

I have no idea where I'm going to put the urn. It doesn't quite fit the décor of my condo. And do I really want my parents' ashes hanging around?

great way to listen to the music. □ There used to be all kinds of music. Sometimes even lyrics in front of it. Once, some hidden

Naked

I have a question. A simple question. A one word question that contains every other possible question. It can be asked sharply. It can be asked softly. It can be asked as a plea or a casual thing without gravity. I've had it before and it disrupted my sleep. I've had it before and not been able to eat. I've had it before and ignored it until it went away. I don't know why it always returns. I've never had the courage to explore its depth. I've always feared its answer will be complex.

I raise my hand the way I was taught in school. I'm alone in my room wearing slippers and a T-shirt. I stand by the window, but no one looks up. I practice asking my question with different inflections. I do this in my head without moving my lips. I drink some water. I refuse the impulse to jump up and down. I don't squirm. I wait patiently with my question, hoping I will get a chance to ask it.

My arm is getting tired and nothing is happening. I leave my room and walk to the subway. I use my last token to get into the station. As I get on the train, my hand hits the top of the doorway. People hear it smack the metal. They see my hand and look away. It hurts, but I keep it raised. Today I am determined to ask my question. I know in my heart that I am not the only one who wants it answered. I know that as soon as I ask it, others will say: "Thank you for asking such a good question."

I am standing on the street in downtown traffic. People in cars are honking their horns. People walking by are averting

behind it. But not hidden so well that I couldn't hear them. They described this place where candy fell from the clouds. And animals

their eyes. My fingers are numb. It's starting to rain and I'm getting cold. I wish I wore pants to keep me warm. I could have lowered my hand to put some on, but I really want to ask my question. It's an important question.

I look up at my hand as I walk through the crowd. My fingers are purple and will not move. My arm looks short and out of place. No one else has their hand raised. No one else has a question. I know this means my turn is next. I will get to ask my question. A man turns away and starts to cough. A woman hands me two dimes and a quarter. My shoulder is aching and my neck is sore. I want to give up and forget my question. But I also want to know the answer. I want to learn. I just have to wait.

It's getting late. There's hardly anyone left on the street. I'm in so much pain, I can barely think. The rain is coming down harder than before.

openly cross-bred in the fields. And anyone at any time could walk on their hands without being stared at. □ Yesterday I pushed the

A Better Way

After the muscles in my neck stopped working, I had to hold my head up with both hands. I would walk down the street with my palms pressed firmly into my temples, my elbows pointing out, left and right. People gave me strange looks, and children would stare and point until they were told they were being rude. Friends continually asked if I had a headache and wouldn't believe me when I assured them there was nothing wrong with my head.

"It's my neck," I would tell them, and they would nod and explain that their necks too, often affected their heads. They would tell me what pills to take and which herbal remedies to use and encouraged me to practise yoga and Tai Chi and Pilates. They would recommend chiropractors and massage therapists, acupuncturists and reiki practitioners. Some suggested Feldenkrais teachers, feng shui consultants and a host of other specialists they were sure could fix me up.

Everyone wanted to give me a business card of someone they guaranteed would make me right. Unable to use my hands to take these cards, I would graciously refuse their well-meant gestures. But inevitably, they mistook my politeness for pride and always found a way to get me to take the cards. My more sensitive friends would slide them into my breast pocket or gently tuck them into the waistband of my pants. Most of them simply pushed them between my lips, smiled and told me to hang in there.

top button on the panel beside the door. It'd been a long time since I even dared to go near that wall. Someone once told me that com-

Onward I walked, my arms getting tired, mouth full of business cards. Every time I passed a garbage can, I was tempted to spit them out. But that didn't feel right. My friends were only trying to help. I owed it to them to keep the cards, to at least hang on to them for a while, even if I never used them.

Eventually, comfort conquered loyalty. I had to swallow or wanted to smile. I felt compelled to speak even though no one was listening. I spit the cards out. A terrible guilt made me feel absolutely awful. I was ashamed, and embarrassed by my shame. I hid my face by rotating my shoulders and pressing my elbows together in front of my nose. This, it turned out, was a better way to hold my head. With my arms covering my eyes, it was difficult for people to recognize me, and I was blissfully unaware of the pointing fingers and strange looks I was still, no doubt, receiving.

Unfortunately, it also made it nearly impossible for me to see where I was going. I would trip on discarded pop cans and sheets of newspapers blowing across the sidewalk. I would bump into

puters in satellites orbiting the earth record the fingerprint of every finger that ever touches any of the buttons. □ That was back when

Phlip Arima

lampposts, people and doors that didn't automatically open. I couldn't trust my footing and my elbows were getting bruised. People were swearing at me, and telling me where I should go, and I was continually apologizing and changing directions until I didn't know where I was or where I was going or where I'd been.

I was frustrated and angry. Just because I had to hold my head up didn't give my friends the right to force their beliefs on me. It wasn't fair of them to put me in a position that made me feel embarrassed, made me have to hide my face. I used to like my face. Now I never get to see it. There were still plenty of mirrors for me to look in, but I didn't want to risk seeing someone watching me. I didn't want to see a stranger looking at me as if I was stranger than anything they'd ever seen.

Finally, I'd had enough. My arms were aching and my legs were unsteady. I lay down on a park bench and stared up at the sky. It was filled with clouds that shifted and churned and disappeared behind tall buildings. Lightning struck and thunder hurt my ears. Sticking my fingers deep inside them, I realized this might be an ideal way for me to hold my head.

I sat up to make sure I was right. My thumbs hooked naturally under the top of my jaw. It was a better way to support my skull. The thunder was muffled and I was sure I wouldn't be able to hear anything anyone had to say. Best of all, I could see where I was going, but could easily shift my other fingers over my eyes and not have to see anything I didn't want to look at. My arms still got tired, but back when the muscles in my neck originally stopped working, I realized it was useless to ever expect anything to be perfect.

they didn't say anything. And if they did, it was always a complaint about the weather. □ I had to try three times before I jumped high

Dead Company

It never chirps. It can't. It's dead. A cricket. Or the shell of a cricket, there might be nothing inside. I've never seen it alive. I keep it in a matchbox—a tiny cardboard drawer—one that once held forty sulphur-tipped wooden sticks. It doesn't anymore. I keep it on the floor not too far from the mattress. The mattress is dirty. I think it's dirty from me living on it.

From its edge come little bits of foam crumb. They get even dirtier—dark like the stuff in the cracks in the floor. Then they disappear. Disappeared is different than dead. The disappeared can't be kept. The kept however, can disappear. I hope the cricket doesn't. Company, even quiet company, is important.

When crickets far away chirp and are many and loud, it's night. Right now they're quiet, so it must be day. Day is when the sun can come out. Once, while I was watching a movie, this happened. I was surprised when it arrived. It came out from above the mattress. It sat on the floor near the wall. I invited it to watch the movie with me. I told it what had already happened, explained that the movie was about a man who could breathe under water. It didn't say a word, just moved along the wall until it reached the corner. Then it disappeared. At least I think it disappeared. It might be dead.

The man in the movie wasn't supposed to let anyone know he could breathe under water. But because he needed company, people found out. This made his life very complicated. If he had

enough to reach the button. I was able to watch myself in the full-length mirror. I looked pretty athletic. It made me want to play a

disappeared, he probably could've kept it a secret. Of course, if he could've kept it secret, he probably would have disappeared. He would have been like the man in this book I once read. He didn't have any company. He hadn't even ever seen the sun. When he disappeared, no one knew he had ever been. It was like he *never was*. Being *never was* is better than being dead. *Never was* means no one knows you aren't. To be with dead company is like being the man in the book. I think it's also a bit like being able to breathe under water.

Last night, when the far away crickets were many and loud, I ate a peanut. It didn't have a shell. It was just the part from inside. It was raw and dead. At least, I think it was dead. It was definitely very very quiet. The man in the movie could've learned a lot from that peanut. I wonder if he ever tried talking with a peanut. I wonder if peanuts taste different under water. I used to roast them to make them taste different. I never used more than one match per peanut. Sometimes, if I held the match in just the right position, the peanut would hiss. Never once did

sport. It wouldn't necessarily have to be a jumping sport. It could be a bending or crouching sport. I don't think I could do a running

Philip Arima

any of them ever chirp. That was before I ran out of matches. It didn't take long for them to disappear. I think maybe this was supposed to happen. Otherwise, where would I keep the cricket?

The stuff in the cracks in the floor never gets washed away. It never moves. It never chirps. Like the sun, it doesn't ever say a word. I don't think it will ever disappear. If I could disappear, maybe I could breathe under water. I wonder if the sun ever comes out under water. To find out, I'd have to disappear to a place with water. The cricket wouldn't mind. It doesn't breathe. The mattress doesn't either, not even from its edge. I think I'm the only thing that breathes.

My peanuts might breathe, but I don't know that much about them. I've never tried talking with them. I don't consider them company. I do, however, always keep them well away from the edge. It's not that I'd mind them being close to the cricket, but I don't want them to get too dirty. I don't want to confuse them with the stuff in the cracks in the floor. I also don't want them to turn into little bits. I don't want them to disappear. Food, even

sport. I live in an elevator. □ I think people stopped visiting me because the music stopped. Though it could've been the other way

food that isn't company, should always be easy to find.

If I could chirp, I wouldn't feel so dead. I might be brave enough to leave the mattress. I would get away from the edge and the disappearing little bits. I would walk across the cracks in the floor, go over to the wall and look for the sun. I might even go far away and learn to be loud. Maybe, far away, I would find forty more sulphur-tipped wooden sticks. I would again be able to make my peanuts hiss. I wouldn't have time to wonder what it's like to breathe under water. I wouldn't want to disappear. Before long, I would have a second matchbox. Probably, I wouldn't ever be at risk of being *never was*.

around. Some days I think it's one way; on others I think it isn't. The truth is, I don't know that much about music. I've never had

Phlip Arima

Seizure

A thirty-eight-year-old man with receding hairline wearing a blue blazer over beige pants and gripping a briefcase climbs the steps of the TD Centre. He fits in perfectly with the people on their way to work. Looking up at the dark towers, he feels himself slip. He falls to the ground. The muscles in his neck constrict. His face hollows and turns pale. His limbs flail. His eyes tear. His deep moan turns heads his direction.

A woman, slightly younger than the man, strides across the pavement. She pushes through the people staring at the stricken man. Dropping her briefcase, she kneels down beside him. She reaches out to hold his head. As soon as she touches him, her body spasms. She rolls onto her side. Her eyes dilate. Her limbs flail. Her body shakes. Her high-pitched shriek joins his.

More people stop to see what is happening. Several pull cellphones from their pockets. One man, taking off his jacket and tie, moves forward and touches the woman. Immediately, he joins the pair on the ground. His body convulses. His hands beat the pavement. His head jerks from side to side. His animal cry is added to theirs.

A thick crowd surrounds the three struggling individuals. No one seems to know what to do. Several people exchange frightened looks. One man, frozen where he stands, monotonously repeats: *oh-my-god, oh-my-god, oh-my-god*. A woman near the front declares:

fuck this, turns and flees. Others follow her lead as more people push to see what is happening.

An old man dressed in rags parts the crowd. He is bent and dirty. He smells. Putting his bags down, he surveys the flat faces watching the spectacle. He considers the people on the ground. With obvious effort, he straightens, looks up at the sky and raises his hands above his head. Taking several deep breaths, he gathers his strength. Then, as he sinks into a crouch, he emits a long drawn-out command. Louder than the shrieks and moans that fill the air he shouts: *Yeeeeeee—WORK!*

The two men and the woman stand. Without looking at one another, they brush the dirt from their clothes, pick up their briefcases, walk into the crowd.

nothing. Just stale and dark. Then I noticed a far-off glow. A faint red that said: *Exit.* As I watched, it got brighter and bigger. It was

Waiting for a Friend

I'm waiting for a friend, watching the faces go by. I look into their eyes, hope for a smile. Glazed or preoccupied, each and every one keeps moving out of sight. I study the creased face of an old man. As he limps closer, I try to send out a good-natured vibe. He looks up at my face. I start to smile. Then the blast of a car horn breaks my concentration. When I look back, he's already passed me. His back is bent and his neck is sunburnt. He isn't much of a man anymore. Probably wasn't much when he was young.

I look at my watch. It's way later than I thought. I wonder why my friend isn't here. I could wait another ten minutes or get on with my day. It's sunny and bright and there's a slight breeze keeping it cool. Three little girls walk by. One of them has a jump rope. I say hi, ask if they're going to the park to play. They look at each other but not at me. I try again, "Beautiful day for skipping rope." They start to walk faster. I shout for them to have fun. They start to run.

I walk in the direction I think my friend might be coming from. The woman ahead of me is holding the side of her head. I catch up to her just as she turns the corner. I hear her voice. It's strong and confident. The phone in her hand is as small as a television remote. Right behind me, I hear a man shout, "Hey, hello." This might be my friend. I stop and he bumps into me. He gives me a dirty look. He isn't my friend. His cellphone is smaller than the woman's.

like a train coming through a tunnel. It came with a wind in front of it. □ I started to get excited. I was ready to jump from the elevator

I go into a pub and sit at the bar. Everyone is talking to someone about something. I scan the room. No one looks the least bit like my friend. One by one, I look at each face. Something is wrong with every one of them. Eyes too wide. Nose too long. Mouth just a little bit too small to relax. Then I hear a voice say, "Hi. How ya doing?" I can hardly believe it. There's a man right beside me asking me a question. "Alright," I say, turning to face him. "How are you?" He answers and asks what he can get me. I tell him I'm waiting for a friend. He says that's alright and to shout when I'm ready. Then he takes off around the bar and starts pulling drafts.

I don't start shouting. This is a civilized place. Sooner or later my friend might be here. It's the kind of place where we would be comfortable meeting. I wish he would hurry. I just have to be patient. When he arrives, I know we'll have a real cool time. We won't even have to talk. We can just hang out and relax—people-watch or whatever. Two friends doing nothing, just enjoying each other's company.

and greet it with words I remembered from the lyrics. Things like: *Love, love me love,* and *Yes, yes only you,* and *Of course, of course*

Philip Arima

I feel like I've been waiting forever. Bored, I hit the street. It's better to be moving. If I keep walking, I'm way more likely to find my friend. Besides, my butt was getting sore. I shouldn't have to wait so long for a friend. If I was a liar or a user or cruel, I could understand it. But I'm none of those things. Oh, I know I'm not perfect. My fingers are too thick. And my ears are too small. But deep down, I'm not shallow. I can be generous, kind. I always laugh when someone tells a joke.

Some men are gathering at the corner. They start to laugh. I wonder what they think is so funny. Their laughter seems forced, unreal, like they're only pretending to feel something they think they should. They keep slapping each other on the back. People steer clear of them, walk faster as they pass. Some women join them and give each one a hug. They don't laugh anymore. They look up and down the street. Then one of them points and the whole group walks away.

I look at all the people on both sides of the street. I peer into every passing face. None of them are the same size or

I'll always be true. □ I imagined great worlds spreading out in front of me. Glittering cities alive with animated mouths. Vast fields

shape. Every other person wears head-phones or dark glasses. Like me, a lot of them are walking alone, but they all seem to know where they're going.

purple with eggplant. Lapis and platinum skies pregnant with rain that smells like laughter. □ I realized I was holding my breath.

Philip Arima

Yucky

"Wow, excuse me," he dances off his bicycle and calls to the woman he nearly ran down.

"Yes?" she says, turning to face him.

"You've got a great smile," he tells her as he pushes his hair out of his face.

"Is that a pickup line?" She smiles again and he pretends to look bashful.

"Well, content-wise it's a compliment.

But depending on your response . . ." She takes note of his chest, biceps and thighs. "Yes, it could be utilized as such."

"And how do you assess my response?" she asks, crossing her arms under her breasts, forcing them up into prominence.

"Well," he says, rubbing his chin to see if he remembered to shave. "Again, content-wise, it's a bit guarded. However, it is a question that could be construed as encouragement for further conversation. Yet, it isn't an acknowledgement of the compliment, so it might best be interpreted as a challenge—a challenge I might be inspired to face."

"But if you consider the other aspects of communication," she says, closing the distance between them, "the ones that subtly—sometimes blatantly—enhance the purely verbal . . ."

"Posture, facial expression or expressions," he lists as he crouches to lock his bike. "Voice intonation, inflection, pitch." He hopes his teeth are clean. "Gaze direction, stillness/movement, eye contact or lack thereof."

Realized I was getting light-headed and trembling. Suddenly I was incredibly thirsty. I think I was thirsty enough to drink the weather

"Not forgetting," she continues, "breath rate, pulse rate, perspiration and/or other secretions such as pheromones, saliva and possibly tears."

"Then I would have to say, your initial response was antagonistic." He looks up from her high-heeled sneakers and falls in love with her silver tights.

"Antagonistic?" She pouts. "That seems rather severe. Cautious would be a much kinder assessment."

"However . . . " He stands. "As I was about to continue, this caution faded in a nano-second of unconscious thought and was soundly replaced by an interest, a curiosity—if you will—as to how I might respond or even react to your response."

"So, returning to your earlier comment." She sits down on the bench next to his bike. "Are you going to take up the challenge?"

"That all depends." He joins her on the bench and casually stretches his arm around her. "I must first consider the possible merits of such an endeavour."

"Do you know what the challenge entails?" She slides her hand down her short skirt allowing it to brush against his

my visitors complained about. □ But I knew the *Exit* would lead me to water. Knew it would take me to places I'd never imagined.

leg. "Or might entail? Or could entail?" She turns to face him. "Do you even know what the challenge is?"

He lets his fingers touch her shoulder. "The challenge I've chosen might be different than the one you expect me to accept."

Delighted, she wiggles and says, "Then you've concluded that the possible merits are worthy of your efforts."

He likes the feel of her skin. "The challenge—its existence, shape, texture and nature—depends more on my desire than yours. But in answer to your other questions, your *mights* and *coulds* perhaps will be actualized or diminished according to circumstances that shall become apparent if relevant to the success or failure of my endeavour."

"So," she attempts to clarify, "according to your framework, desire drives challenge." Her arms are covered in gooseflesh. "Would you say desire is the foundation on which this conversation commenced and continues?"

"If we recognize that my compliment was the end product of a desire to share my opinion—yes." He looks up to the

Knew I would know the unknowable if I stepped from the elevator. Left the fan behind. Left the wall-to-wall carpeting. The full-length

right and considers his thoughts. Then, taking a deep breath, continues. "Even if we wish to take it a step further back—to your smiling at me." He smiles at her. "And recognize that as a form of communication." He is pleased she is also smiling at him. "And given it is safe to assume a desire inspired it, that is to say, drove you to smile—then again, yes, as far as commencement is concerned."

Sighing, she nods, so he keeps talking. "As to this conversation's continuation and in particular my participation in its continuation, a primary consideration is the possibility that your agenda and/or desire or desires may exclude mine."

"In which case, you will be left with a dead pickup line." She giggles. "An unreciprocated gesture, to be polite." She reaches up and strokes his hand. "A bite and some pointless reeling in, to be metaphorical. To be blunt, a memory of unconsummated innocuous superficial foreplay."

"Negative," he rallies, "for the first. And your metaphor implies I cast a lure and this has not been satisfactorily established." He lifts his arm from around her

mirror. □ I let go my breath. The now bright red glowing *Exit*, bigger than big—went dark. Gone. Everything instantly complete and

Philip Arima

45 ←

shoulder and takes her hand in his. "While the last claim assumes a yet-to-be demonstrated knowledge of how my memory functions."

"Which leaves the second," she says.

"Which leaves the second," he agrees. "A politeness—a shallow sentiment—I prefer to think of as an unappreciated compliment."

Twisting her body away from his, she counters, "Not necessarily unappreciated. Do you honestly believe appreciation requires acknowledgement or reciprocation for its existence?"

"Without the former or the latter—which implies the former," he stands and feels himself swing loose in the cavernous crotch of his jeans, "the existence of appreciation cannot be known." He lights a cigarette. "This in turn, begs the question: does the unknown exist insofar as the ignorant are concerned?"

"Ignorant you may forever remain." She gets to her feet and looks down the street. "But I could tell you something you really should know."

He sucks on the cigarette. She starts to walk away. The cigarette glows.

total black. And stale. Oppressively frighteningly stale. □ Then the door shut. ∎

"Smoking is yucky," she says, and does not wave goodbye.

I Am Dreaming: silhouettes of light, people as negative space on a dark canvas of thought. I talk. My words are soft—more pigment

Philip Arima

Chicken
Noodle Soup

—City-wide domestic help desk, Rick speaking. How may I assist you? —Thank gawd. I've been like listening to that awful muzak for ten minutes. —Yeah, it's pretty bad. Sorry to have kept you waiting. —Why'd it take so long? —McDonald's' workers went on strike today. The phones haven't stopped ringing. They say it could last a while. —

That's awful. There should be a law. Like with hospitals and the fire department and stuff like that. —I couldn't agree with you more. —Really? That's like, so cool. Most people never think I know anything. —That's hard to believe. You sound so . . . so . . . I don't know . . . together. —Really? You're so sweet. What's your name? —Rick. And you are? —Heather. —Heather, that's a pretty name. Heather. —Thanks. You're so . . . so . . . sweet. —So what can I do for you, Heather?

—I'm like starving. I went out and got a can of soup, but I don't know what to do with it. —Condensed soup? —I don't know . . . hey yeah, that's what it says. — Well Heather, there're a lot of things you can do with it. What did you want to make? —What do you mean Rick? I'm starving! I wanna make soup! —Okay Heather, stay calm. We can do this. You and me together, alright? —Alright, it's just . . . it's just . . . the directions are so complicated. —I know. But don't you worry. We're a team now. —You're so sweet. —So are you. —Really? —Oh come on, I betcha you get told that all the time. —No I don't. Not like really. Not by

than sound. I can't make them full. I can't give them shape. They don't colour the people I dream—the two dimensionals all around me. The people who really like, mean it. —I think I know what you mean. —Really? Wow Rick. I betcha you do. —Sure I do. Most people only say it 'cause they want to get something out of you. —That's it. That's it exactly. It's 'cause of how I look. —I betcha you're real pretty. —You're so sweet. —So are you.

—Rick? —Yes Heather? —I'm like really really starving. —Right…okay…yeah …let's get started. —What do I do? —First off, what part of the directions don't you understand? —Well, like right here, where it says to empty the contents into a saucepan —Okay Heather, I'm sure we can do that. —But Rick, I don't know what a saucepan is. —Oh honey, you're so sweet. Saucepan is just a fancy word for pot. —Then why don't they just say pot? —I really don't know. Maybe they just like making things difficult. —That's so mean. —It certainly is. —So what do I do? — Have you got a small pot? One that's a little more than twice the size of the can? —Rick, I do. My mother gave me one for my birthday. I use it to water the plants.

—You have plants? —Oh yes. I've got all kinds of them. —That's so cool. I love

edge of my perception, a solid frame. The volume control part of some other game. I reach out my hand to touch one who is close. It

plants. —Really? Wow. —Only, mine keep dying. And then I have to buy new ones. —Me too Rick. Me too. It's like I'm always spending money on new plants. —Sometimes . . . Heather, sometimes . . . I think they make them so they'll die. That way we have to keep buying more and they make more money. —That's so mean. —Yeah. Especially since all we want is to make our places a little nicer. —Exactly. Though even without plants, I have a pretty nice place. —That's nice Heather. You're really lucky. —I betcha you'd like my place Rick. —Especially if you're there. —Really? Wow. You're so sweet. —Do you have any pets? —No. I hate animals. —Me too. But Heather, do you want to know a secret? —If you wanna tell me. —I do. —Okay then. —I once had a goldfish. —Really? —Only it died. —Like the plants. —Exactly. — They're so mean. —Yeah.

—Rick? —Right, you're starving. — Yes, but I . . . I . . . — Okay, have you got your pot? —Yes. — Okay. Now you have to open the can. —Alright. —Do you have a can opener? —No. —No? . . . oh Heather, this is so . . . oh . . . I mean, this

passes through her middle without resistance. It sharpens and flattens when in her light. I study my skin. I can see every line and pore and isn't . . . its just that . . . —Rick! Rick, it's alright! It's alright. I got the kind with the pull tab lid. —Thank gawd. I thought we were in trouble there. —Hey, I'm not stupid. —I know you're not. Heather, I think . . . I think . . . —Yes? —I think . . . I think you should open the can and pour it into your pot. — Oh . . . okay. There. Done. — Alright now, what kind of soup is it? — Chicken noodle. —Heather, that's my favourite! —Really? Wow. —Yeah. —Mine too Rick. —Wow. —Yeah.

—Okay Heather, the rest is simple. — Good. I *really* am starving. —I know. But we're almost there. We're a team. —Rick and Heather. —No, Heather and Rick. The pretty should always come first. —Oh Rick, you're so sweet. —So are you. — And the soup . . . —Is salty. —Hey, that's funny. —Yeah. Heather, I'm having so much fun. —Me too Rick. —But back to business. —Okay. What do I do now? — Like I said, the rest is simple. Fill the empty can with water and then pour the water into the pot. —Hot or cold? — Good question. I knew you were smart. —Thanks. —It doesn't matter. —What do you mean it doesn't matter? It does so!

clinging hair follicle. They are foreign and frightening. Their definition dissolves as my hand re-enters the dark. □ The right side of my

Philip Arima

Stupid people are . . . are so . . . so . . . I don't know . . . they're . . . —No, honey, sweetheart, the water. The water doesn't matter. Hot or cold, it makes no difference. But if you use hot, the soup will be ready faster. —Oh, I'm sorry Rick. I thought . . . I thought you were . . . —It's alright. — You're so sweet. I'd like to . . .

—Okay, Heather. Now all you have to do is put the pot on the stove and turn the burner on low. —That's all? — Well, you need to stir it every now and then. — Why? —So the noodles won't stick to the bottom of the pot. —I can do that. — Heather, I know you can. —How will I know when it's ready? —When it starts to bubble, it's ready. —Really? —Yeah. And then you won't be starving. —Rick, I can hardly wait. —It won't be long now. — You like saved my life. I really can't thank you enough. —Well, Heather . . . —Yes? —I was wondering . . . —Yes? —I was wondering if maybe later . . . —Yes? —I was wondering if maybe later . . . —Yes? —If it's alright to ask, you know, privacy respected and all that . . . —Yes? —And understanding that you don't have to answer if you don't want to . . . —Yes? —

body is numb. I feel a glue hardening my eyes. I hear something drip. It happens again and then there is silence. I listen intently, wait for

but, I was wondering what you're doing after you eat? —Nothing special. Well, just one thing. —Oh ... well then ... never mind. Sorry to have pried. Enjoy your soup. I'll be ... —No, Rick, don't hang up. —What? —You wanna know a secret? — If you want to tell me. —I do. —Okay. — After I eat, I have to throw up. —Really? Wow Heather, me too.

more. The silhouettes lose some of their brilliance. The drip sounds again three times in a row. In the silence that follows, I say a word. It

Philip Arima

55

Togetherness

She and I are walking down the street. All I have to do is turn my wrist and our hands will touch. It would feel good to have my skin against hers. I imagine her taking my hand in hers, imagine her nails gently digging in, her dry palm getting moist, her slender arm tensing as we twist and slip and sidestep down the street.

People are looking at us. She's chic in a leather skirt and silk blouse with pointy-toed boots kissing her knees. I'm casual in pleated trousers and a sports shirt of the palest blue. Her hair is blond, short and gelled into a perfect imitation of esprit. Mine is dark, pulled tight across my scalp into a braid that hangs down my back. Separate, we look good. Together, we are stunning. We're the best looking pair on the street.

I see her glance at me without turning her head. I must be staring. I tell myself to watch where I'm going, keep my eyes on the sidewalk. I just can't believe we're walking down the street together. I'm in a city full of strangers and we're so close. I think she just smiled. She must be sharing my thoughts. I let the moment colour me with a glow that starts in my stomach and swells in my throat.

She stops at a window to look at a jacket. I step out of the flow and lean against the next building. As people stream past, I take off my dark glasses and polish them clean. Hardly anyone's wearing a jacket and everyone looks healthy and alive. Two young women,

has no colour and makes no sense. The two dimensionals move into the distance. Static and nothingness. I feel the coming from opposite directions, smile at me. I smile back, but have no intention of pursuing either opportunity. I can afford to be friendly. I'm happy waiting.

She decides the jacket isn't for her. Just as well, since I don't really want to go shopping. I just want her and I to walk down the street. Her energy merging with mine, no hurry and nowhere I have to be. It's at times like this that I'm sure something great is going to happen. She and I are moving toward a climax.

We reach a crowded corner and wait for the light to change. We're pushed into one another and I can smell her perfume. It's musky with a hint of citrus and something I can't identify. I close my eyes, inhale and let my shoulders relax. I start to drift and my head tilts back. She and I are the only two people in the world. We were made for one another and nothing should ever come between us.

I cross the street a few steps ahead of her. I can feel myself starting to strut. Huge buildings look down at us. Fast cars race past. Heavy trucks shake the earth. But I am invincible. I turn to tell her how I feel. I want to let it all out, let it engulf us.

frame closing in. Drip again. A puddle of pain around and in and through my brain. Darkness. The solid edge. I clench my hand into a

Philip Arima

I want to see her as high as me. I want us to fly beyond the mundane.

She's half a block away. When we crossed the street, she went south down Bay. I'm still standing near the corner, wondering what to do. Should I keep heading east or try to catch up to her? She's slowing down. She's stopping. She's looking around. Turning around. I see her smile and wave her hand. She's coming back toward me. She's speeding up. Her whole body's in motion, fluid and flowing.

She's kissing some guy I didn't see.

fist. A thought turns to action. There is a crash. □ I open my eyes. The floor of the elevator is covered in shards of broken mirror.

The Music Lover

The piano player walks into the tavern just after nine o'clock. The bartender is mixing his drink before he sits down. Taking a sip, he nods his approval, but she has already walked to the far end of the bar. He glances at his watch and decides to order a chicken sandwich. It's a typical Thursday night: a crowd of loud men at the bar obsessed with the large screen television, students at tables shouting to one another, women laughing, couples hiding in the shadows. The bouncers are relaxed and joking with one another.

He finishes his drink as the bartender places another in front of him. "Chicken, toasted brown," he tells her, and she again walks away without a word. They have little in common and nothing to talk about. The longest conversation they ever had took less than five minutes. Even on the nights when she comes home with him, they don't pretend there is anything between them.

The sandwich arrives with a coffee. He opens it and looks at the dry white meat. He pokes it with his finger and looks at the bartender. She is again at the far end of the bar. He pushes the sandwich away and swallows some coffee. It's burnt and cold. He lights a cigarette, but after a few drags cannot be bothered to finish it. Putting it out in his coffee, he sighs and goes over to the piano.

A young man is standing beside it. He is well-dressed and alone and looks as if he eats three meals a day. The piano

There's a small part of me in every piece. My hand is throbbing. My body, stiff. Anxiety grips. I realize I cannot remember my name. I

player feels shabby in his discount clothes. He should have shaved before coming to work. The man says hello and shakes his hand. The piano player tries to remember how to smile. Giving up, he shrugs and sits down on his bench. Undeterred, the young man explains that this is his first time to the city. He tells the piano player he has always loved music and is thrilled to actually be talking to a real musician. He has dozens of questions he asks without waiting for answers. He has ideas he wants to discuss, thoughts he wants to share.

The piano player thinks he remembers how to smile. When the young man stops talking, he manages a grin that makes him look frightened. The young man thinks he has done something wrong. He apologizes and begs the piano player not to be upset. He promises not to ask any more questions. He promises to stay quiet. He promises to be respectful. He even offers to make the bartender turn off the television.

The piano player grins some more and tells the young man to sit down. He opens the piano and places his hands on

make a list of words that seem to sound right. I say them aloud. They hang dull in the silence. They disappear. ☐ I look at the wall which

the keys. He touches them in a way he has never thought to touch the bartender. He murmurs soft words that only he can hear. He is acutely aware of the young man's presence. He takes a deep breath and begins to play.

The piano player's fingers fly across the keys. His feet work the pedals the same way a hanged man's feet kick the air. His head moves in rhythm with the melody. He doesn't think about the students only interested in drinking. Laughter does not disrupt his focus. His shoulders rotate and his body sways. Sweat wets his face as he slides without break from one song into another. He doesn't hear the buzz of the countless conversations. He is oblivious to the men more interested in sports. He closes his eyes and hears the words he longs to sing.

He is playing better than he has ever played in his entire life. For once it doesn't matter that the piano hasn't strings. He is not saddened by the fact that the music he plays is only in his mind. He is not angry that his effort is without effect.

Afraid he'll never be this good again, the piano player doesn't want to let the set end. He plays non-stop for over an hour. When finally exhausted, he lifts his fingers from the keys. The young man is on his feet. He applauds and shouts, "Bravo! Bravissimo! Encore! More!" Everyone in the tavern turns and stares. The piano player rushes to the bar and downs a drink. He asks the bartender if she will come home with him when she finishes her shift. The young man joins them and repeatedly kisses the piano player's hands.

The young man is so excited he can't stop shouting. He tells the piano player he loves him more than anything else in the world. He begs the piano player to teach him to play. The men at the bar tell the young man to shut up. They tell him they don't like his kind in here. The young man tells them to go to hell. A student throws a beer bottle and a fight begins. The bouncers move in and break it up. The young man is thrown out. The bartender answers the piano player's question.

my eyes and the shapes come alive. They move and shimmer and turn in on themselves. With nowhere to go they crowd toward me. □

Intimacy

"Can I spit?" I ask, looking down from the top of the tower. She looks at the sign that lists the rules. *No Spitting* is third from the top. "Sure, go ahead," she says, "but you'll never know who you hit."

"It's not that I want to hit anyone." I feel accused. "I just want to spit, watch it fall, break apart, disappear."

"Then go ahead. Let her rip."

With both hands on the railing, I lean over the edge. She presses against me, wraps her arms around me. I like the way her body feels. I like her hands on mine. I shiver and squirm and tilt my head toward the ground.

"Do it," her mouth is near my ear, the side of her face in my hair. Our thighs seem attached. Her hands repeatedly contract. "Spit."

I let it drool from my mouth. It extends into a long single drip. I part my lips. It falls, breaks apart, disappears.

Pain pierces my sinuses. It moves into my forehead and vibrates my temples. It intensifies in my eyes then penetrates my brain. I stand. I

All the Same

It's a medium-size city: small enough that people smile at one another on the street; large enough that not everyone knows everyone else. It's a safe place with strangers who are all quite similar. Hairstyles are conservative and clothing, functional. Rough language is never heard and drunkenness never seen. Everyone speaks only one language and no one has an accent different from any-one else. Neighbours may occasionally quarrel, but grudges are never held. And not one single teenager has ever consid-ered committing a crime. It's widely accepted that there isn't any reason for domestic disputes, emotional, physical or sexual abuse.

There are five different kinds of house a family can choose to buy. Built on neat plots of land exactly two-hundred-fifty-six meters square, each house is of equal value and has a mortgage that will never change—a mortgage that can never be fully paid. In the summer the lawns are kept putting-green perfect, roses are grown and chemical pesticides are never used. There's no litter on the street and everyone recycles. There isn't any noise after eleven at night except on New Year's Eve when festivities continue to twelve forty-five. In the winter the snow is removed as it falls. And should anyone's car ever get stuck, there's always a crowd of people rushing to help.

There is only one design of condo-minium—for those who prefer that kind of lifestyle. And each unit is guaranteed

sway. I tighten the muscles in my arms and legs. I slowly turn around, see only walls. Looking at the door, I will it to open. When

never to depreciate nor, under any circumstance, appreciate. All of these modestly luxurious complexes feature a fountain directly in front of their large double doors. They each have the right number of squash courts for no one to use, and are clustered together at precisely planned intervals around the perimeter of the downtown core. They each have a swimming pool, whirlpool and weight room that are cleaned every day by well-paid staff who never complain. The grounds, which are painstakingly cared for by unseen gardeners, are constantly patrolled by exceedingly friendly handsome guards. All the windows—none of which can ever be opened—are always immaculately clean.

It is a regular functional place to live. No one is terribly rich and no one is horribly poor. Vagrants, policemen and drug dealers are never seen. Some teenagers leave, but are never referred to as runaways. Singles only socialize with singles. And families only socialize with families. Everyone who has a job works a reasonable number of hours at a pointless occupation they consider themselves fortunate

nothing happens, I step again. And again. My ear to the door, I listen and wait. A few moments later, I hear a soft drip. ■

Philip Arima

to have. Those who don't work, do so by choice and are content to spend their days telling themselves how lucky they are to live average lives that are empty of crises.

Fathers in this medium-size city repeatedly tell their daughters to be good girls and save themselves for marriage. They stress the virtue of purity and innocent thought. They trust their love is enough to inspire their daughters to do as they're taught. They tell their sons, often in the same breath, to experience all the wonders the world has to offer, to be uninhibited, virile, brave and manly. The daughters, shy and frightened of confrontation, never dream of disobeying. They stay sweet and chaste and constantly anxious. The sons, terrified by the possibility that they might disappoint their fathers, do everyone they can as often as they can—morning, noon and night. They too are constantly anxious.

The mothers, which is to say the wives, since no one who lives there is ever separated, let alone divorced, make sure their daughters never do anything their fathers won't be able to understand. They read private letters and diaries. They

It Seems There is a hole. It's small and all alone. I've never seen it before. It's up near the top of the elevator where the ceiling meets

listen in on confidential phone conversations. They follow their daughters when they go to meet friends at the mall. They do all these things without any guilt. They do them in the name of motherly love. And each and every night, they bemoan to their daughters the awful duty of *putting out* for their husbands. They patiently explain that it is a dirty pain. They sagely counsel in conspiratorial tones: "Don't give it away until you find *mister right*. And never touch yourself except to wash and check for cancerous spots."

For the boys the mothers do a great deal more. They meet them after school and between dinner and dusk to teach them every carnal pleasure they've ever imagined. The latter they accomplish by signing up for government-subsidized night courses and joining bridge clubs and volunteering their time on committees with long convoluted names. Then they never attend a single thing. And since there are so many sons—so many to be done—they encourage their husbands to go bowling, play friendly penny-ante poker and sign up for government-subsidized night courses.

the wall. It's close to the corner farthest from the door. It's dark. And it's quiet. I don't know where it goes. I'm not sure it knows I'm here.

Philip Arima

The husbands are not at all chagrined to do as their wives suggest. They go out most nights to accommodate their spouses. But instead of pursuing innocent activities, they gather in small groups to watch pornographic videos. Laughing and cheering, they break up the monotony by complaining that their wives never do the things they are watching take place on the screen. And since this grows tedious, they often exclaim with self-righteous venom: "I'd never marry a girl who would ever do anything as disgusting as that." Then they wish there was a prostitute they could regularly visit and perhaps keep as a private mistress.

Now the singles in this medium-size city that will never appear on the front page of any national newspaper, live basic lives they hope they can proudly say are decent and just the way they should be. The single men, like the family men, watch pornographic videos. However, since they are ashamed of their lust, they watch them in private and never admit they have the slightest interest in such base entertainment. Younger and stronger than their married counterparts,

I don't know that it cares. □ I'm crouching with my heels flat on the floor. My chin is on my knees. My arms around my legs. My neck

and commanding a greater disposable income, they also go bowling and play penny-ante poker and spend money on books they need for the government-subsidized night courses they regularly attend with dogmatic determination.

The single women dutifully work at jobs they plan to quit as soon as they find *mister right*. At night they stay home carefully studying bridal brochures, wedding magazines and catalogues that feature silver and crystal and the finest china. Some learn to knit and others to sew. And they all make sure they can cook several healthy meals suitable for a family with two-point-five children. Since these women are still the obedient daughters their fathers so puritanically raised, they only go out on Saturday night. And, remembering the advice their mothers so guilelessly bestowed, they always insist their dates take them out to overpriced restaurants where they can safely flirt with no intention of ever saying good night with anything more than a coy peck on the cheek.

Everything is quite fine in this medium-size city. It's a safe place with strangers

aches. I am watching the hole to make sure it doesn't disappear. I don't know why it would. I don't know that it will. It seems quite content.

who are all quite similar. Everyone is depressed, but not one single one of them would ever believe it. The mother-wives are the least likely to go mad, disappear or suicide. They only feel vulnerable when they look in the mirror.

It might even be happy. I would like to ask it how it got here. □ A long time ago I used to talk. I could voice my thoughts. Ideas would

Pickled **M**ango

The wind blows the blind from the window, letting overcast light penetrate the bedroom. Sibbie wakes. She mentally traces the tension from her limbs up her back and into her neck. She looks at the ceiling and sees cobwebs in the corner. Sighing, she rolls over and realizes her husband has turned into a pickle. Contentedly snoring, immersed in a dream she cannot imagine, he lies inert, dark green and bumpy. A pungent dill assaults her nostrils. Surprised but not shocked, Sibbie touches the preserved vegetable dominating the far side of the bed. Her hand comes away wet and slimy. She raises it to her lips, but cannot bring herself to take a taste.

Lyle, sensing a finger on his throat, wakes. He gets out of bed—a pickle in pajamas standing erect. He runs a hand across his stubbly face and looks at his wife—a mango with eyes blinking shut, rapidly ripening red. Confused, he goes to the bathroom and gets in the shower. As the steaming water washes over him, he slowly returns to his former self. He wonders when Sibbie changed and if she is sweeter than the woman he married. He gets out of the shower and shaves. He puts on his most expensive cologne and goes back to the bedroom to ask his wife if she knows she's turned into a mango.

Sibbie's in the kitchen making coffee. Lyle gets dressed and finds her in the dining room reading the morning paper. She is no longer a mango. She is the woman he lives with, supports and

come to me and I would play with them. I could undress them and take them apart. I'd put them back together differently than they'd

complains about. She hands him the sports section and says good morning. He kisses her on the cheek and pours himself a cup of coffee. They make toast and eat in silence. Sibbie laughs aloud when she reads an article describing a patent dispute over genetically altered fruit. Lyle doesn't notice. He's engrossed in a story about hockey players who believe eating cucumber seeds will make them better athletes. Sibbie goes for a shower and puts on fresh underwear.

An hour later, their daughter phones to tell them her television has turned into a garden. They tell her it's nothing to be overly concerned about. They advise her to let it grow naturally, agree that pulling the weeds is okay, but that under no circumstances should she use any pesticides whatsoever. She thanks them and hangs up. The phone rings again. It's their son calling to tell them his television has turned into a garden. He's already chopped down every single plant and is taking a breather before digging up the roots. Sibbie and Lyle plead with him to leave them alone. They explain that the plants might grow back, thrive and flourish.

been. I would re-dress them so they appeared better than they were. My neck is changing. Its message is listening to my body. I am □

Phlip Arima

But their son is determined to finish what he's started. They get in an argument and the call ends badly.

Sibbie takes Lyle's hands in hers. They look into each other's eyes for the first time in years. They see fear. Lyle looks down at their hands. His are green and starting to sweat. Sibbie runs to a mirror and watches her skin slowly smoothen. She presses her hands against the pulpy mass of her forehead. She feels it give. Lyle is at the door putting on his coat. Sibbie joins him and together they walk out into the street. They head for the ravine a few blocks away. They notice many other couples close to their age walking in the same direction. Sibbie waves to Audrey, one of the members of her coffee klatch. Lyle shouts hello to her husband, Steve. Both Audrey and Steve quickly look away. Lyle and Sibbie pretend they don't care, keep holding hands and continue to walk with the fast growing crowd.

Sibbie and Lyle are half way down the ravine. The earth is soft and sucks at their feet. Their balance is off and their progress slow. A dozen steps later, they

numb. The ache's in my legs. My arms are heavy. The outsides of my feet and all my toes are tingling as if burning in ice. Something in my

cannot continue. They are firmly planted where they stand, surrounded by thousands of couples equally confined to small plots of land. It starts to rain. Sibbie and Lyle watch people transform into plants. They see sycamores flourish and roses bloom. Two creeping ivies madly entwine. An oak and willow crowd one another. Figs and apples and tomatoes and beans and rice and strawberries ripen. Pollen fills the air and fragrances war with one another.

Sibbie and Lyle shudder. They too are no longer human. They can feel their roots sucking up moisture. But unlike their neighbours, they are not growing. Her voice shaking more than her limbs, Sibbie whispers: "Perhaps ... perhaps it's because you're already pickled." Lyle considers this as Sibbie begins to complain about her feet. Her leaves start to wither and her limbs begin to droop. Watching her fruit wrinkle and drop to the ground, Lyle begins to cry thin tears of weak vinegar. Petrified with fear and not knowing what to do, Lyle thinks to say a prayer. But when he closes his eyes, he forgets the words and suffocates.

back is screaming up my spine. I can't understand what it's trying to tell me. □ I think the hole is big enough for my thumb. It's too far

Phlip Arima

In the Grey

I ordered these lenses through an 800 number I found in the back of a magazine. They were the only permanent contacts I could afford. The ad in the magazine said they were as good as the ones in the stores. Brand name has never mattered that much to me. If a product works, I'm happy. If it looks good, even better. The way I figure it, the fashion machine is

away for me to find out for sure. This is unfortunate. Accurate knowledge is important. Having a use for knowledge is even better. Better

always ripping us off. But if you're smart and keep your eyes open, there's always a deal waiting to be had. When I saw these lenses on TV, I knew they were for me.

A friend of mine—now an ex-friend of mine—helped me install them. I could have done it myself, but I was a bit nervous about getting the interface right. I didn't want to damage the lenses. And I definitely didn't want to end up with some kind of permanent nerve damage. Of course, I was excited too. After all, my vision was going to be better than it had ever been before. I was going to look really cool. Everyone was going to wish they were as kick-ass as me. It was sweet. Really sweet. Though feeling nervous and excited at the same time was weird. I was . . . I don't know . . . unsure I guess. So I called up my friend and talked her into helping me. She's good with hardware and software and anything that's new. I stroked her vanity, promised her dinner and eternal gratitude.

She was really impressed that I got the kind of lenses that make my eyes into mirrors. Jinn-the-Puppet had mirror eyes.

And she and I and just about everyone everywhere grew up on Jinn cartoons. Every character Jinn looked at saw themself the way he saw them. It was funny how shocked they were when they realized who they must be. Then they carried on the same as always, but just different enough that you knew they knew the truth about their place in the world. Jinn was like a demonic god. He could make anybody he wanted into whatever he thought of them. He was always laughing at the end of the show.

The lenses worked great for the first few weeks. Then something went wrong. Every now and then, there would be moments when I couldn't see. It was like I blinked in slow motion. The world would disappear. All I could see was fuzzy colour, like I was staring at wet paint on glass. Then *bam*, the world would be back. After I got over being pissed off that something was wrong with the lenses, it was really trippy. When the total weirdness of it started to feel normal, I really got into the swirling colours as they shrank and expanded, moved and stayed static— hazel to green to both with streaks of the

is something I would like to be. It might give me the confidence to say a few words. □ My body is I would tell the hole it's not alone.

Philip Arima

dullest yellow and sometimes a grey threatening to go black.

The first few times I saw the grey it was pretty scary, but fascinating too. I'd see a small dark dot, usually right in the centre of all the colour. It just sat there, more solid than anything I'd ever imagined. It seemed to be waiting for me to notice it. And when I did, I wouldn't be able to look away. Like a black hole it possessed some great power. I was compelled to look at it. And as soon as I was in its grip, it would start to expand. It would expand until it was all there was. I ceased to exist. I was part of it. There was nothing else and nothing I could do about it. Then it would recede super fast, the same way a camera flash is instantly gone.

My ex-friend wanted to take the lenses out. She said it wasn't too late for the procedure to be safe. She kept warning me that if I didn't do it now, if I let it wait too long, I would be stuck with the lenses for the rest of my life. I told her that would be fine. We got into fights. She said the lenses were malfunctioning, reversing, turning the mirrors into my vision. She said I was going to go blind. I tried to

silent. I can't make it move. Even my eyelids won't blink. I can feel a lump inside my centre. I don't know where it's from, but it's cylindrical

explain that I wouldn't mind being blind. I described the colours and how the grey made me feel like I was part of something greater than anything else. She said I was crazy, said the interface was screwing with my brain. She threatened to knock me out and remove the lenses against my will. She wanted to take away what I didn't even know I'd been looking for. So I cut her out. There was no way I was going to let her deprive me of the glorious grey.

Soon the lenses were blinking out more often than not. I bought one of those white sticks blind people use. I carried it with me everywhere I went, but always kept it folded and hidden in my knapsack. Whenever the colours appeared I would just sit down and trance to the show until the grey came on and made me whole. I started walking the streets with my hand touching the buildings. That way when I went down, I'd have something to lean against. As soon as the world disappeared my knees would bend and I'd be sitting on the pavement, the happiest guy that ever lived. There I'd be, the traffic fading into so much white

and the size of my thumb. It's starting to get hot. It's turning to liquid. □ I hope it will stop if I pretend not to notice. □ I make myself think of

Philip Arima

noise, just barely able to hear people passing by, blissed-out and one, without a worry and no desire.

The few friends I still had were freaked by my eyes. We'd be sitting in a café, or more and more often a bar, and the lenses would do their trick. Everything would be perfect, but they couldn't handle it. They told me I looked like something from a horror film. They said they could see right into my brain; that each time I tranced out, they could see my nerves pulsing slower and slower. I told them they had too much imagination. They said I moaned and talked to myself. I told them they were full of it. They said they were worried about me. But really, they were just jealous. They couldn't understand where I was at, where I was coming from. And they definitely couldn't handle being left out. They'll never understand how lucky I am. I'm free and they're still trapped where I used to be.

Of course, I don't hang with them anymore. I'm freer than anyone's willing to believe. I no longer see anything but the grey and, once in a rare while, the swirling colours. When the nurses tell me I have to

a place that isn't here. I remember an idea I kept to myself. It's light and full, sweet and pleasant. It reminds me of a world without any

go for a walk, I go for a walk. It takes a lot of effort to make my legs work, but I can usually manage it for long enough to keep the nurses from nagging. When they tell me to eat, I eat. But food doesn't really interest me. Sometimes, not too often anymore, hardly ever really, I think it's a shame so many people are trapped in the false reality. Then I zone in on the grey, trance and know I'm okay.

walls. It's flowing from me onto the floor. It might disappear if I take it apart. ∎

Phlip Arima

Trafficked

This island isn't mine. I know it's not mine. It belongs to everyone. But I like to pretend it's mine. I come here every morning before anyone else even thinks to arrive, usually before the sun starts to rise. I sit in my favourite spot, legs crossed, hands resting on my knees. I close my eyes and simply breathe. I feel my body expand and contract with each breath. I let my mind drift with each expansion. I let it wander through my torso, along my limbs and to the end of each finger and toe. I merge with the earth and become one with the air. I feel the cool of night slowly recede. I breathe and become my breath until I see the sun's light through the thin lids of my eyes.

Then I open my eyes. I look out beyond myself. I see the world in which I live. The buildings at the far edge of the city are the first to catch the morning light. Their windows start to glow one floor at a time. Smog creeps up their walls and slowly surrounds them. And just beyond the shore of my island, the buildings close by come out of their shadows. Light from within brightens their windows. I begin to see the outlines of people starting their day. Breathing, still aware of the oneness of my body and everything that is, I watch their silhouettes move in and out of their frames, multiply and return to the duties they left the day before.

The trickle of traffic flowing around my island has gradually increased. The *thrum* of rubber on asphalt is the white noise of

Separate and Alone I cannot move. My feet are still flat to the floor. Also my butt. My knees are bent. My back against the wall. I

life. A sparse progression of people mutely step on and off my island intent on reaching their destinations. Then, like a flash flooding of a desert riverbed, the road is filled with thousands of cars. Screeching breaks and honking horns destroy the lazy morning peace. Crowds of commuters, stranded on my island, brush up against me, press into my back. An occasional voice makes a snide comment. Curses bounce off. Chuckles assault. Once, several years ago, a woman asked if I was alright. She bent down to look into my face. When I didn't respond, she repeated her question. I waited for her to ask again, but the rush toward excellence pulled her away.

I reach between my legs, take hold of my briefcase. In one smooth motion, I stand and lift it from the pavement. I take a moment to stretch my neck. I blink and yawn and straighten my tie. I step from the island into the traffic.

close my eyes, listen. Listen again. And again, deeper. I pretend to hear a ticking. I pretend it comes from beyond my empty. It speeds

Phlip Arima

Blue **D**enim

—Wake up. —Go away. —Wake up. It's important. —What? —Wake up and open your eyes. —Okay, okay. I'm up. What do you want? —Look. —*Oh-my-god.* We're surrounded. —No shit. —When did this happen? —While you were off in la la land. —Why didn't you wake me up? —I did. —I mean sooner. —'Cause it just happened. —Alright, what are we going to do? —I don't know. — Well, think of something. —I woke you up. —Great. Why do I always have to be the one to get us out of these situations? —Would you rather I had just let you sleep? —It would be better than facing this. —Then go back to sleep. —Are you crazy? I'll have nightmares. —Like you don't already. —That's besides the point. —And what's the point? —Look, we're surrounded. This isn't the time for a philo-sophical discussion. —Discussion? When have we ever had a discussion? Argument, yes. Debate, maybe. Discus-sion? Never happens. —Okay, okay. Leave it alone. —Fine. Go back to sleep. —Relax. —How can I? We're surrounded. —I know. —What are we going to do? — I don't know. —Great.

—Where did they all come from? — They just appeared. —Don't be ridicu-lous. —I'm not. I had my eyes closed and . . . —You had your eyes closed? — Well so did you. —You told me to. You said I looked tired and should try to sleep. —And I can't be tired too? Have you got some kind of corner on the market? — No. It's just that . . . look, I don't want to

and slows. It gets loud, goes soft. It dissolves. I imagine myself tall enough to touch the ceiling. It's hard but flexible. When I push, my

argue. We're in real trouble here. —No shit. —Where'd they all come from? I've never seen so much blue denim in one place. —I can hardly believe so many people wear it. —Even my nightmares are preferable to this. —What are we going to do? —Play it cool. —How? I can't stop shaking. —Get a grip. We'll . . . we'll get out of this. —You don't sound all that confident. —I'm just waking up. —Great. When it's time for action, you're stuck in neutral. —I'm thinking. —Don't hurt yourself. —You're not helping. —I woke you up. —Oh, sorry. *Thank you so very much.* —You're so very, *very* welcome. —Look, we can't do anything anyway. We're on a subway train. —I knew we should've walked. —Like you didn't want to take the train as much as me. —I was prepared to walk. —Like a zombie in the dark. —Anything would be better than this.

—Blue denim. —Surrounded. —Repeating the obvious isn't going to help. —You're one to talk. —I'm thinking too. —And I'm not? —How would I know what goes on in your head? —Uh-oh. —What? —They're looking at us. —Be cool. —Stop saying that. —What do you

fingers force it away. It stays that way—extended, distorted, pressed out into the world. □ There's something in my throat. A tiny tickle

Philip Arima

97

scratching. It moves from front to back and around again. And again. And again slowly speeding. It widens and elongates, scratches deeper

want me to say? —Say this isn't happening. —This isn't happening. —Yes it is. — I know. —Great. I was better off with you in la la land. —You'd want to face this alone? —At least I wouldn't have to listen to you. —You want me to leave? —I want us both to leave. —We've got to get out of this. —Do you think we will? —We've gotten out of worse. —I guess. —Sure we have. —This is pretty bad. —But we'll get out of it. —How? —Trust me. —Like I have a choice. —We all always have a choice. —I thought you didn't want to get philosophical? — That's not philosophy. It's a basic truth. —Says you. —Not just me. —Since when do you listen to anyone but yourself? —How long have I been listening to you? —Only long enough to put me down. —Well if you'd say something intelligent I wouldn't have to. —See, there you go again. —Why is everything always my fault? —Why aren't you getting us out of this mess?

—We're slowing down. —No we're not. —Yes we are. —We're in the middle of the tunnel. —So? —So we can't stop here. —Why not? —'Cause we have to get to the next station. —Who says? —I do. —You've been wrong before. —Like you're always right. —That's not what I said. —But that's what you meant. —No it isn't. —Yes it is. —I woke you up, didn't I? —I could go back to sleep. —Can you look out the window? —Yeah. —What do you see? —We're slowing down. —We're stopping. —We've stopped. —No shit. — We'll start moving again. —It better be soon. —They're not going to smother us. —Then why are they moving closer? — They're not. —Yes they are. —You're imagining things. —You wish. —Ignore them. —I can't. —Then close your eyes. —Are you crazy? —It'll work. —They're not going to go away just because I can't see them. —They might. —Great. You call that thinking? —Like you would know what it's like to think. —I don't know why I woke you up.

—Thank God, we're moving again. — No shit. —Is that all you can say? —Shit no. —Oh, aren't we witty. —How would you know? You're not even aware of what goes on right in front of you. If it wasn't for me, you wouldn't even know we were surrounded. —Like there's anything I can do about it. —Go back to sleep. —Not

with each revolution. I open my mouth. A fly flies out. I open my eyes, watch it sparkle through the air—a lapis and emerald jewel on

Broken Accidents

just yet. —What do I have to do, beg? —You don't want me to go back to sleep. —Wanna bet? —I've thought of something. —And it's going to work? —Yeah. It's going to work. —This I've got to hear. —When we pull into the next station the doors are going to open. —Did you have to do research to figure that out? —Do you want to hear my plan? —This is a plan? —I'm laying the groundwork, so you'll understand. —I'm not stupid you know. —I thought you didn't want to debate. —I thought that word was beyond your vocabulary. —My vocabulary has words that can describe you better than you know yourself. —Crass monosyllables are nothing to brag about. —I wouldn't waste my time bragging to someone who can't understand what I'm saying. —I understand more than you know. —Do you think you can grasp the subtleties of my plan? —With my eyes closed. —When we pull into the next station the doors will open. —I got that part. —And maybe they'll get off. —That's your plan? —No. That's a possibility. —Not likely. —You never know. —Do you even know what station's next? —How

translucent wings. I watch it circle the elevator. I watch it rise. It nears the ceiling. It hits the wall. □ I close my mouth as it falls. I want to

can I? I was asleep. —Might as well still be. —I'll just ignore that. —You just failed. —Starting now. —Whatever.

—Do you want to hear my plan? —There's more? —I told you, that was just a possibility. —More groundwork? —If it wasn't necessary, I wouldn't have to do it. —It's not necessary. —Like you're in a position to judge. —I can see myself better than you know. —Yeah, sure. But self-delusion doesn't help. —And you're helping? —I've got a plan. —So you say. —You don't want to hear it? —How long have I been waiting? —I could let you wait longer. —Get on with it. —After the doors open, we let whoever might get off, get off, and we let whoever might get on, get on. —I hope you didn't hurt yourself figuring that out. —Then we wait until no one's in the door. —You did hurt yourself. —We'll hear the signal that the doors are about to close. —I thought you had a plan? —And when they start to shut, we'll make a run for it. —That's your plan? — Got a better one? —No. —So who's stuck in neutral now? —I came up with the same plan ages ago. —Then why didn't you say something earlier? —I

move to catch it but my hands are fixed to my knees. My arms are solid tubes of bone and muscle and sinew. I close my eyes, hear its

wanted to see if you were bright enough to figure it out yourself.

—Ready? —Ready. —Let everybody get off first. —I know. —Wait till the door is clear. —I got it the first time. —We're going to get out of this. —No shit. —Another battle won. —Victory. —Give me a kiss. —I love you. —I love you too. —Wanna hold hands? — Okay. —Let's not fight anymore. —Okay. —We can just hold hands for the rest of our lives. —Whatever you want. —I want us to have children. —Wait for the signal. —I will. —*Oh-my-god.* —The platform's full.

wings move the air. I feel a drop of sweat travel down my ribs. Another tickle scratches my throat. I open my mouth. Another fly flies

Dropping **O**ut

Microwaves distort. So I rig the oven door and put my head inside to zap the thoughts I don't like. My heart stops. Dead, I go for a walk. I meet other dead people. We agree it's a drag and decide to go hitchhiking in the rain. We don't really care where we end up. We just want to keep moving, maybe find a place where we can talk to some people who

out. I imagine the two of them circling. I hear them hit the walls. I imagine them as they fall. I close my mouth. Open it. A fly flies out.

live. Maybe, if we're lucky, we'll learn to believe we're alive.

Far off, we see some dark clouds. We run to intercept them. Rain may not be falling from them, but they're the best bet we have. Several people drop out after only a few minutes. I try to encourage them, tell them that even if the clouds aren't raining when we get to them, they eventually will. They tell me that if we wait in one place long enough, raining clouds will inevitably pass over. I can't argue with this. They're right. But waiting's not for me. I want to start hitchhiking as soon as possible.

I know I have to learn to relax. Maybe I should take up some kind of meditation. I'm going to go crazy running around chasing clouds. But there are these thoughts in my head goading me to do irrational things. Once, I found myself talking to the television when it wasn't turned on. Another time, I spent an entire afternoon practicing my signature using a name I'd read on a milk carton. I don't know where these thoughts come from. I don't even know if they're mine. Sometimes I worry that whoever owns them will invoice me for their use and I won't be able to pay them without incurring interest.

More people drop out. They've decided they don't really want to hitch-hike in the rain. It's too romantic. They tell me they're going to get jobs in fast food establishments. They hope that if they work hard and keep their opinions to themselves, they'll one day get to stand at the *drive-thru* windows. I tell them this is an achievable goal and wish them luck. They urge me to join them, but I'm too afraid to make the commitment.

There's only myself and one other person running for the clouds. This may be a good thing. A huge group wasn't likely to get a ride. People often hitchhike in pairs. Pairs are acceptable. Perhaps a driver will think we're a couple. Couples aren't as threatening as singles. There was a couple living in the apartment next to mine. Whenever we met by the elevator or at the front door they said hello. I'd say hello back. And if there was time, we'd discuss the weather—the likelihood of rain.

Three in the air. They hit the walls. I open my mouth. A fly flies out. Open mouth. Fly out. Open, out. Open out. . . . □ The elevator is loud

Phlip Arima

Yawn

Once upon a time in the many tomorrows of yesterday, a giant jaw opens to yawn and lets forth a sound syrupped in a flavour never before tasted by dawn or dusk or brilliant daylight. A cup of filtered water evaporates as silence tries to return. Radio static warps the aura of trees more than ten feet tall. The dark hours begin, pretend they'll not end. And in the mind I still possess, a cough answers the yawn, but chokes on itself so isn't heard.

Imagine a starless night sky murmuring secrets to creatures living in deep caves where lurid adventures are commonplace and bodily sounds sacrilegious. To burp like a child is considered a sin. To fart during sex, a heretical act. Grinding teeth while asleep indicates a lapse in devotional practice. Allowing them to chatter might be overlooked, but there is no guarantee the noise will not drive loved ones insane.

I see ten thousand million trembling fingers slide into pink ears when common emotions are whispered aloud. They get stuck and make perfectly healthy hair appear full of split ends. Sneezing is messy. Hugging impossible. And drinking café au lait on fashionable patios requires a heat-resistant straw. Turning a hand into a fist, slapping—or clapping for that matter—are fantasies that can never be fulfilled. Elbows in eyes make most of the population look like raccoons.

In my pocket I have a purple computer that resembles a pet rock. When I use it near trees the screen is brighter. It has a

with wings moving air. A constant static. I listen as the flies hit the walls. An intermittent rhythm builds. I cannot move. Time takes

built-in microphone for recording secrets and I have programmed it to assess the relative value of everything it understands. If I tell it to play dead, it asks if I want to exit. This is a question I can only answer when the parameters of remaining are accurately translated into a language comprehensible to chameleons and sleeping sloths.

I climb a tree to get closer to the sky. A man on a bicycle rides underneath me. He's listening to a play-by-play commentary of a National Hockey League playoff game. No one is winning. There are leaves in my face so all I can see is shimmering green. I think there is an ant crawling into my pants. It feels quite large and seems in a hurry. I wonder if it's red or black and if it has wings. Where it might fly I cannot imagine. This might be a good thing, since I think I have a tendency toward paranoia.

The sun goes down and stars want to come out. I can't see the comet the newspaper said is on its way. I fall out of the tree and walk down the street, move through the city, search for a silence that will cure my cough. An absolutely white space. I open my eyes, see ten thousand flies. They circle, collide. I focus on one as it passes close. Its wings are a blur. Its legs hang

plate with a diameter greater than my waist hovers in front of me. On its pristine edge teeters a moldy fortune cookie. Knowledge I have subconsciously kept from myself is making my stomach grumble. I turn to my right and enter another moment. People on a bus from a mall and from inside a television are staring at me. If the police are alerted, I will be arrested.

I blink and mysteriously drop through the pavement into a nursery. Diapered infants in their cribs have their eyes tightly shut. Lights flash on and off. Another cup of filtered water evaporates. A glossy magazine in the window of a corner store turns into a billboard advertising masochism as an advantageous career move. I misplace my bank card so must dip into my loonie collection to purchase toilet paper, mouthwash and mascara.

stiff. I see it as alone, separate from the rest. It hits a wall—adds another tick to the rhythm—falls. I close my eyes, open my mouth.

Just Me

—We think it will be better if you remove your head. —But I already took off my face. —True. And it's an improvement. But your head is still in the way. —In the way? How can it possibly be in the way? In the way of what? —In the way of our thoughts. —But it's *my* head. —Our head. —Yes, but I use it more. —That's debatable. —You want to debate? —

You'll lose. —Still … —Remove your head. —But I need it. —Are you sure?

I give up. I take off my head, *our* head. Arguing with myself is pointless. I always give in. It's foolish to prolong the inevitable. Arguing in the singular with me using *we* and *our*, the plural of potential, how can I win? There's just one me and so many of *them*. The committee of ass-holes. The *they* that never give in. But this time I'm pretty sure I have them. Without my head, where will they live? Where else is there enough empty space?

—Twit. —You're calling me a twit? I took off my head. You should be dead. Can you feel yourselves dying? —Twit. — I am just me. And you are soon no longer going to be a *we*. —Twit.

It's always like this. If I get ahead, or they think I might get ahead, they get abusive. They taunt me with names. *Twit* is one of their favourites. *Dum-dum, fool, nerd, silly-billy*, I've heard them all hissed and hollered, moaned and sighed, plainly stated, painfully screamed, laughed, cackled, even coughed. But from now on, no more. I'm done with my head. *They* cannot be. *Them* is dead.

Fly out. □ Slow, I swallow. All sound ceases. I open my eyes. The elevator is empty. ∎

—Twit. —Okay. I give in. Why am I a twit?

Now they won't answer. They won't say a thing for a good long while. It's part of their game. The silent treatment. They're waiting for me to implode. Then they'll call me a name. All I have to do is stay calm. If I let it all go, I know they'll vanish. Whoosh, gone, conceptual evaporation. Yet I can never quite manage to get them completely out of my mind. For some absurd reason, I always try to understand.

—Silly-billy. —Why aren't you dead? — Dum-dum. —Where are you? —Fool. —You can't be in my heart. It's too small for your thoughts. And you've always said my guts are unstable. My legs are too solid. Probably from all the time I spend running from every last one of you! — Nerdy-nerd.

I know this part of the game too. They want me to figure it out without their help. They always have all the answers. But to simply explain the what of *that* and the this of *what* isn't enough. They want to laugh at me as I try to work it all out. *They* are not very kind. Not very fair either,

Looking Within The elevator is shrinking. Or I am growing. The ceiling is closer. The walls not so distant. My feet take up most of the

since they are many and I am just me with only one brain—a brain I abandoned when I took off my head.

floor. The buttons on the wall are larger than my eyes. I feel my hair flatten against the top of my skull. The door is small and getting

Wireless

I search myself to find out who I am. I link from site to site. I get lost on the highway. I see data displays cascade down the page. I'm not who I thought I was. I'm a small section of thread that is part of a network. I'm a bit of debris the size of a fingernail hitting a satellite as it circles the earth. I'm a sponge in the ocean waiting for a wave. The shore is more than a lifetime away.

I obsessively play Nintendo till dawn. I miss all my Monday night programs. I'll have to phone a friend to find out what happened. I go to the store to get a phone that works. I stop at the bank machine so I can buy a really good one. It swallows my card and won't give it back. I hit it and the man on the floor tells me he's trying to sleep. I tell him I know the feeling.

If people were human, what would happen to all the liposuction machines? This is a question that keeps me awake at night. When I ask my tarot cards for an answer, they tell me to be patient and eat more broccoli. Instead, I drink coffee with cream. I pretend I'm a painting on a wall in a beautiful frame. Every five decades I get sold at an auction. My value goes up and I'm always insured.

I have a tape measure I use to determine the breadth of my ideas. The numbers are small and covered in rust. The rust flakes off and gets embedded in the carpet. When I vacuum I forget everything except what my mother told me: "Watch what you're doing and go over every spot five times." She also told me to always dust first.

smaller. ☐ I bend and crouch. I think of sports I've never played. I curl tight into a ball. Space continues to condense. My elbows connect

It's difficult to reach the back of my closet. The light keeps burning out and it's full of sealed boxes. They're stacked to the ceiling and too heavy for me to move by myself. I labelled each one with a cheap magic marker. Over the years the ink has faded.

When I see advertisements for pepper spray I get sexually excited. I keep meaning to get some, but I'm afraid I might develop a habit. I might end up having to go to anonymous meetings. I'll have to be honest about my feelings. I might start believing in God. Or worse, I might stop being afraid of people.

Last week I didn't receive any mail. I was expecting an eviction notice, a copy of *Newsweek*, *Gun and Rifle* and a lingerie catalogue. If they don't arrive soon I might have to file a complaint.

with the walls. The hole is close to my face. I shift my head so my eye is in line with it. It's now too small for me to see where it goes.

The Importance of Sunglasses

Well yes, I'm certainly aware that some people see it that way. My mother always told me: "There are as many opinions as there are individuals." However, even though I've been part of his personal entourage for over three years, I haven't the seniority to make a significant impact in the direction his image will take. You must remember, I'm just one of forty-two people who never leave his side—and only the top two or three really have any understanding of what he's all about.

He's big. His videos are seen on screens around the globe. There isn't a single week that his picture isn't on the cover of at least five magazines. His music is played in churches and jails, kindergarten classrooms and business boardrooms. His lyrics are quoted at the dinner tables of suburban homeowners. He's a multi-billion-dollar corporation with influence in every major sector of society. And his fan base is second to none.

It's been just over six weeks since I was promoted to my present position. Actually—off the record, just between you and me—some people consider it a demotion and think I should take a cut in pay. Not that this would bother me. Nor, for that matter, do the opinions of those little people bother me either. It's just internal politics. My present responsibilities are just as important as my previous ones. They're just different. I mean, honestly, every little detail any member of his personal entourage takes care of is incredibly important. That's why we're his

From it I feel an ancient wind. □ There's something crawling up my spine. I cannot reach to slap it. I wish it would fly into a nothingness.

personal entourage. It's petty to poke at one another about rank and pecking order.

Anyway, to answer that last question: *yes, without me, it is quite possible his public image would suffer*. I have been entrusted to ensure that there is always a clean pair of sunglasses ready to replace the ones he's wearing whenever he feels they need to be changed. I have this custom-designed case full of sunglasses. Just look at the size of it. It's almost as big as his guitar case. Inside this are three pairs of every style of sunglasses he wears. Minus the pair he's got on right now of course. Whenever he takes off his sunglasses, I slide up next to him and we make the switch as effortlessly as a groupie taking off her clothes.

Now I'm not one to brag, but I'm pretty good at what I do. I've memorized all the subtle hand signals he uses to tell me when he wants to change to a different style of sunglasses. And I haven't given him the wrong pair once. Needless to say, there hasn't been a single streak or smear on any of them. And, I think there's only been two photographs of us making a switch. Of course, he knew I was a ringer

I tilt my face toward the floor. My head is pushed between my knees. Each thread of the carpet is as thick as my thumb. I am mesmerized

Philip Arima

121 ←

for this position. Believe me, he knows how smooth I can be.

I'm so happy he's letting me be responsible for something where my skills are seen by the media. I'm now an obvious part of his public image. Without me he wouldn't look right. And to be totally honest, I've wanted a more public position for quite a while. It's really cool to see pictures of myself standing next to him in magazines. My mother's so proud of me. Now she can tell all her friends how important I am. She was never really comfortable with me being the one who rolled on his condoms.

by their convoluted interaction. I focus on one and its colours separate. I realize its whole is only parts. □ The crawling thing is at the top of

Entertainment

At three a.m. I sink my teeth into my skin. I watch the blood begin to flow. Tam, sitting across from me, also watches. The blood seeps across the table. It fills the initials carved in the wood. It looks like syrup. The candles flicker.

Jean comes out from behind the counter to see what we're doing. She pulls up a chair and waits for the wound to clot. The street beyond the window is quiet, the room dark. The candles flicker. We don't talk.

The café door opens and a young couple come in. They're too well-dressed for this part of town. They come over to our table. As the man sees the blood, the woman says, "Gerald, I don't think this is our kind of place."

We look up. I smile. The woman chokes. Gerald rushes her out the door. The candles flicker. The blood clots.

my neck. I want to scream. It moves to my ear. I feel it enter and disappear. I open my mouth. Nothing comes out. The wind from the hole

Punk is Beat

Jimmy comes in pushing his feet ahead of him, scraping the heels, toes barely touching the floor. Self-conscious about his height, he habitually stoops and keeps his knees bent. His jeans are faded grey. His ripped T-shirt, sleeveless and stained. At the counter he nods and puts out his cigarette. He orders a coffee and loads it with sugar. The music from the radio hurts his head. It's mid-afternoon and Jimmy just wants to drink his coffee.

Tyler waves from a table in the back. Jimmy doesn't know if he's up to talking. He figures it won't kill him to say hello. Yawning, he crosses the room and nods his head. He looks at the girls sitting with Tyler, also gives each of them a nod. Tyler bounces up and down in his seat, grins. "This is Jimmy. He's from the old school of punk." Jimmy sighs, rubs his scalp. "Fuck off," he says, and yawns again.

"See," Tyler slaps the table. "What did I tell ya?"

The smaller girl, Allison, laughs. Jill, the one with tattooed earlobes, is unimpressed. She lights a cigarette and can't stop coughing. Jimmy takes it from her and she starts to object. He looks at her and she shuts her mouth. Tyler laughs. Jimmy tells him to fuck off, takes a drag from the cigarette and looks at Allison. She smiles and looks away. Jimmy turns around. The floor creaks. Pushing his feet in front of him, he walks to a table close to the door.

A few minutes later, Allison joins him. She offers him a cigarette. Jimmy

circles my body. I force my mind to follow its progress. Together we travel a mystical journey. We touch sensations locked in my skin. We

accepts. They smoke and Allison tries to start several conversations. Jimmy listens, sometimes answers her questions with a shrug. She doesn't give up. She keeps switching topics, hoping she'll find something they have in common. Finishing his coffee, Jimmy yawns. He stands and thanks her for the cigarette. She looks at her hands. She looks over at Tyler. She looks up at Jimmy and asks if she did something wrong.

Jimmy just shrugs and pushes his feet out the door.

scratch the surface of my face. We slide over my tongue and down my throat. Unspeakable knowledge enters my spirit. □ I relax my

Phlip Arima

Answers

—Are you alright? —No. —What's wrong? —Another channeller. —Again? —Yeah. Almost every day. I'm getting tired of it. —Can't you block them out? — Wish I could. —Maybe you should see someone? —Like who? —I don't know. A doctor? Maybe a shrink? —Right. I can hear myself now: "Hey Doc, I got this problem. These freaks from another dimension keep interrupting my life to ask me questions about other people's lives." —You don't have to say it like that. — They'd lock me up. —Maybe not. They might believe you. —Right. —They'd want to study you. —That's the same as being locked up. —It might help. —Being locked up? —Having whatever's happening to you studied: observed and figured out. —Get real. —I'm serious. What's wrong with study and observation? — They wouldn't want to help. They'd want to make it worse so they'd have more to observe. —Well then, how about talking to a psychic? —Same thing. Plus they'd be jealous.

—Uh-oh. —Are you alright? —Do I look alright? —You look worse. —Help me to a chair. —What's happening? — He's breaking through. —Fight it. —I can't. —Try. —What do you think I've been doing? —I don't know. I thought he went away while we were talking. —They don't go away. Once they've got a link, they work it until they get some answers. They get paid for answers. That's what channellers do. —So give him some answers. —It's not that easy. —Why not?

bowels. Gas is released. The elevator expands. I am floating alone in its centre. I start to rotate. The walls spin past. I straighten my legs

—They want the right answers. —That's impossible. How are you supposed to know what goes on in their dimension? We don't even know what goes on around here half the time. Why can't they be satisfied finding things out as they happen? —Why don't you ask them? — Why don't you? —I have. —And? —They ignore my questions. They only want answers. —So give them answers. —It's not that easy.

—Are you alright? —It's getting worse. —I'm worried about you. — Thanks. —Anything I can do? —Hold my hand. —Shit. —What? —I can feel him. —Let go. —I can't. It's like he's right inside my head. —You're telling me. — What a freak. —I know. This guy's one of the worst. Real persistent. —A real nag. —Yeah. He won't stop until he gets some really good answers. —Like what? We don't know hardly anything about anything he might think's important. —We don't even know where he is or who he's channelling for. —Except that it's a woman. —You picked up on that? — Yeah, but that's about it. —Usually is. — This is weird. I can hear some of their

and lift my hands above my head. My speed increases. The walls blur. Their corners dissolve. The elevator screams. I visualize a word

Philip Arima

131

thoughts. —Depressing, aren't they? — Pretty petty existence. —Almost as bad as ours. —What do you think he charges? —What difference does it make? He's not going share it with us. — Like he could if he wanted to. —I don't think he'd want to, even if he could. — What's he think we are, independently wealthy? Nothing better to do than sit around waiting for him and his freak clients to ask us stupid questions?

—I'm starting to get a headache. — Me too. —It'll go away when he breaks the link. —Can't we break the link? —I've tried. It doesn't seem to work that way. — Then let's give him some answers and go have a drink. —Sounds good to me. Tell him what he wants to hear. —How do I do that? —Just keep making things up until he's happy. —That could take a while. — Tell me about it. —What do you think would happen if we told him stuff so out-rageous it couldn't possible be true? — He'd probably love it. —No really, I'm seri-ous. Don't you think he'd think we're nuts and stop bothering us? —I was serious. He'd eat it up. He'd go public with crazy stuff. Make a huge name for himself. Rake

in glowing red letters. □ I stop. □ I'm still in a silence. The elevator door is before me. The buttons are still beside it. I reach out my hand

in the money and feel smug and superior. —Yeah, you're probably right. I betcha he'd even manage to get his face on the cover of a magazine. —No doubt. And he definitely wouldn't give us any credit.

—Let's tell him he's going to be impotent for the rest of his life starting next week. —Hey, I like that. We could also tell him his client's going to lose all control of her bowels. —Especially during sex. —And that they're both going to grow hair on their tongues. —I don't think they'll believe that. —No, I guess not. —It's gotta be something he'll think is possible. —Well then, how about we tell him there's a way he can change the future? —You mean not go impotent? —Exactly. —You've got an idea? —It's brilliant. —Let's hear it. —We'll tell him the only way he can keep from going impotent is to have sex right now. —With the woman he's channelling for. Brilliant. —What did I tell you? —We can tell him she's not going to go for it no matter what he says. —Even better, we can tell him he has to say he's doing it for her own good. —So she'll be able to go on enjoying sex. —She'll scream rape. —She'll scream it to the

and my arm elongates. I take ten deep breaths and blink my eyes. I feel a finger touch a button. A light goes on. The door slowly opens.

media. —He'll be famous. —He'll be infamous. —He'll get his face on the cover of a magazine.

I rest a hand flat on my stomach. I put the other on the back of my head. I feel a connection. I feel a pulse, a question.

The Key

He knocks on the door and hears no sound. He knocks again. Silence. The sky is overcast. His raincoat, new. He's the only person on the street. Without thought, he kicks the door. It's like slamming his boot into a wall. Undeterred, he kicks the door three more times. His last effort produces a sound similar to a fist sinking into a pillow. Staring at the door, he waits. His shoulders slump and a slight bend appears in his back. Reaching into his pocket, he pulls out a key and slides it into the lock. It turns without a sound, but the door remains shut. He sighs, repockets the key and walks down the steps back to the sidewalk. Looking over his shoulder, he sees the door open. It is no longer a threshold he wishes to cross.

When he reaches the next house, his coat is weathered. His boots have lost their polished gleam. The day is darker and his hair has grown. He looks at the shuttered windows high overhead. He mumbles a prayer, closes his eyes and straightens as much as his back will allow. Knocking, he hears an echo. It repeats several times then abruptly stops. A persistent wind blows from the street. Saliva gathers at the corner of his mouth then drips down his chin. He knocks again. He wipes his face. He kicks the door and waits. His hands start to shake. He lifts the key close to his face. Its metallic surface is duller than plastic. He easily slides it into the lock. It turns and he hears the mechanism click. He leans his weight into the door. It does not shift.

Exiting the Elevator I walk down the hallway. Its long and bright and lined with dark doors. The one at the end is lit from behind.

Back on the sidewalk, he watches the door swing open. He shakes his head and shuffles down the street. He moves as if every muscle in his body aches. His hair turns grey. Wrinkles distort his face. The street stretches out before him, block upon block of desolate houses. His thoughts repeat, fragment and repeat until they lose all meaning. He's still the only person on the street. The wind turns cold. His eyes start to water. Cracks in the pavement fill with dirt. The streetlights come on, but make little difference.

The next door is the same colour as the previous two. It looks brand new. Painfully, he lifts his hand to the door. He knocks. It sounds the way he thinks it should. He knocks again, and again it sounds the same. Waiting, he wonders if anything has changed. Wanting to kick the door, he tries to lift his foot. Disappointed, he looks down at his feet and sees that his boots are nothing but tattered strips of leather—soleless and useless.

The key turns in the lock. He hears the bolt disengage. It starts to rain. The key rotates to where it began. Around and

Except for it, each door has a number where its handle should be. The numbers on the left are odd. On the right, even. Their values increase

Phlip Arima

around he turns it as fast as he can. A machine gun-like rattle shoots from the lock. He stops. The street is dark. The door won't budge. His head involuntarily shakes. Unchecked drool stains what is left of his collar. He unconsciously lets his bladder release. From the sidewalk, he hears the door open.

Lightning flashes. Thunder sounds. He throws the key into the road. It bounces once, hits the far curb and disappears down a sewer. A door appears before him. It slowly opens. He wills himself forward. His vision blurs. His chest contracts. He feels his knees begin to buckle.

the further I move away from the elevator. □ In front of each door is a newspaper. I look at each one as I pass. None of them has a name.

Without a Splash

Bluegrass muzak plays on the line connected to an automated switchboard somewhere in Kansas City. My headset sinks deeper into my ear. I turn a tight circle, grab the hand beating my head. A cigarette, untouched, burns to a stub. Coffee spills from my mug. In the mirror there is sunshine. I look at the hand in my hand, hit it hard against the phone. The bluegrass goes dead. I immediately wish I had something to listen to.

Sitting beside a cactus with long translucent spikes, I watch a flame lengthen in an antique lamp. There is an open book face down on the floor by the bed. I don't remember if I was reading it. Children in the park make noise on the swings. I hit the redial again.

A warrior walks away from a battle. The war is far from being won. As he wanders the land he discards his armour. Naked, with only his sword in his hand, he comes to a river flowing smooth in a silence. He marvels at how it seems not to change.

In the city where I live landmarks never remain. Developers demolish, rebuild and demolish. A hobby designed to generate profit. New restaurants, offices, homes, recreations. Mirrors and flames and children replaced.

After weeks in the silence, the warrior steps forward to cross the river. The sky turns to smoke—purple and swelling. Every cricket in the land begins to chirp. The warrior's feet stay on the surface. His body, erect, does not get wet.

The line is now busy. So much for Kansas City. I pick up the book and stare at the white space between two paragraphs. It wrinkles and roughens and takes on the topography of a snow-bound valley. Deep down in its middle a cigarette ash silently disintegrates.

Halfway across the river, the warrior realizes himself. He drops his sword. As it breaks the surface, the sky turns blue. He sinks into the water. His hands shoot up over his head. His fingertips are last to go under the surface.

right have headlines announcing chemical disasters, automobile and space shuttle accidents, the latest death toll in wars I did not know

Had Enough

—So you want some of mine? —If you have enough to spare? —Sure. —How much do you want for it? —You'll be doing me a favour by taking it. —Really? —Yeah. —That's generous of you. —Not really. I've got too much. —Still, to give it away for free. — Oh, it'll cost you. —I thought you said . . . —Only I won't profit. —I don't understand. —You will. —

When? —After you've had enough. — What if I can't afford it? —You won't have a choice. —Will I be able to sell it? —I don't think so. —Why not? —No one would want it. —Because it's used? —It's all used and reused and passed back and forth over and over again and always. And no one wants the least little bit of any of it. —I want some. Not much. Just enough to help me fit in, be like everyone else. —You only think that now. Once you have some, you'll keep getting more and, like everyone else, you'll wish you never had the least little bit. —Why? —Just the way it is. —You expect me to believe everyone wants to be like me, to not have any of it. —That's right. And the worst part is that none of us can remember not having it. —That's ridiculous. —Perhaps, but it will seem totally reasonable once you've had enough.

  —If I don't like it, I'll just throw it away. —Can't be done. —But you can give it away. —Not really. —I don't understand. —I'm not surprised. —Tell me how you can give it to me and still keep it at the same time. —It's like this: I've got way too much, everyone has, and I can give you

were being fought. ☐ The carpet is white and so brilliantly clean it hurts my eyes. When I look where I've stepped there is no evidence of

some, but that won't diminish mine. — You're not making any sense. —This entire conversation doesn't make sense unless you know what we're talking about. —We're talking about you not sharing with me. —But I am sharing with you. I'm giving it to you as we speak. And the longer we talk the more you're getting. —All I'm getting is frustrated. — There you go. —I didn't ask for frustration. —Many shapes and many forms. Different weights and consistencies, sizes, styles, even different colours. — Oh, aren't we the cryptic one? — Bitterness. —What? —Now you're getting bitter. Sarcasm gives it away. —So? —So now you've got more than just the little bit you wanted. —I don't like it. —Aw, poor little boy doesn't like his new toy. — Who's bitter now? —I don't deny it. —You like it. —I measure everything against it. Everything that doesn't hurt, I know relative to it.

—Will it never fade? —Never. You're stuck with it now. —It hurts. —It'll keep hurting until you don't know how you stand it. —I don't want it to hurt. —You'll spread it around to everyone you know

my passage. The hallway behind me extends out of sight. With each step I take, the pile deepens. With each step I take, the hallway dims.

and everything you touch. —It hurts so bad. —You're just like the rest of us now. —I want to be like I was. —Don't worry, there will be moments like that. —When? —Probably when you won't notice. — That's cruel. —Pity. —Pity? —Yeah. Now you've got it as bad as me. —I'm a fast learner. —Congratulations. —Save it. — Touchy. Touchy. —Piss off. —There there, you'll get used to it. —I don't want to get used to it. —Betcha can't think of anything else. —There isn't anything else. — That's it, now you got it. —Yeah, I thoroughly understand it through and through. —No you don't. —Yes I do. — Don't. —Oh, just because you have more of it, you think you're so superior. — Jealous? —Not a bit. —You can't even imagine its depth. —And you can? —No one can. It has no bottom.

—Tell me something. —What? — Anything. —It won't help —I don't care. —Yes you do. —You wish. —Denial and projection. —Psychobabble. —Next you'll start blaming others. —It's your fault. —You're so lame. —You gave it to me. —Pathetically predictable. —Well you did. —You asked for it. —I didn't know

I try to pick up one of the newspapers. My hands pass through it as if it is light. I try again but my feet have taken me beyond the door. I

what I was asking for. —That's no excuse. —You took advantage of me. —Hey, even without me, you had it coming. —I might've escaped. —Hindsight delusion. —Shut up. —Blame, blame. Whine, whine. Pity, pity partier. —Please. Don't I have enough to deal with already? —There's always more. —Well keep to yourself. —I can't do that. I'm just over-flowing with it. I'll never be happy until every one has as much as me. —I wish I never met you. —Still want me to tell you something? —No. —An ultimate truth? —You got one? —Tried and proven. —Okay. —Any moment of innocence you might actually experience will be spoiled by your fear of when it will end.

cannot stop or turn around. I try again when I reach the next door. My hands pass through as before. I carry on, keep trying. Emotion swells

Phlip Arima

Thirst

I'm wandering through the halls. Some are wide. Some are narrow. Most are straight. The first has carpet. It looks as if I'm the only person ever to step on it. The next is tiled. Then there's linoleum. Then one of wood and one of plastic and others of materials I cannot name. Not a single pattern is repeated quite the same. And each hall is lined with doors. Some have more than others. One has just one even though it is the longest.

Every door is a different size and shape. Most of the doors are beautiful. A few are frightening. Some are ugly. At one point I think I've found a hall with identical doors. I look at each one several times. They all have the same small picture of an overflowing fountain repeatedly carved from top to bottom along one edge. I study the doors with greater care and discover that the number of fountains on each is not the same. On the first there are three hundred and seventy-two. The next, three hundred and seventy-five. Then three hundred and eighty-nine. Three hundred and fifty-six. Three hundred and . . . I stop wasting my time and turn right at the next hall.

I stop in front of a door twice my size. It's metallic blue. It seems to glow and bow slightly outward. Engraved at eye-level is a small design made up of three lines. The longest line turns against itself twice. The other two are so close together they could be one. They cut the first in half. I brush it with my fingertips. My libido kicks. Elation makes me bold. I knock as

each time my hands are in a newspaper. Those on the left produce a joy. The right, hate. □ The carpet is like mud. It rises above my

if I have the right. My effort is muted. The sound does not resonate. There is no acknowledgement of my existence. I try again. My knuckles sting. There is no bell for me to ring. There is no handle, knob or crash bar. I push against it with all my strength. It will not move.

The hall I just entered has no doors. It curves to the right and the floor is slanted in the same direction. Walking feels odd but not awkward. Every few steps I come to a paper clip. They're small and tarnished and bent with use. I put them in my pocket and they are mine. At twenty, they stop. I keep walking, watching the floor. I keep turning my head from side to side, my eyes wide. I speed up and start to sweat. I pass a door that is ajar.

I vaguely remember an old man wrapped in blankets. He's lonely and lost. He's holding my hand as I stand by his bed. I can't keep still. I want him to release his grip so I can go to the toilet. His hand is hurting mine. He tells me he was once loved by millions. He tells me he had power. He lifts his other hand from under the blankets. A shaky fist moves close to my face. Deformed fingers open

ankles. It clings to my feet. As it tops my shins, I fall on my face. The door at the end is moments away. I continue toward it on hands and

to reveal a paper clip. I take it and run to the bathroom. In my hurry to open my pants, I drop the paper clip into the toilet. I flush and hear loud cries. I run back to his room. The door is shut. A stranger stands guard and won't let me in.

I stop near the end of the hall. I take several deep breaths, tell myself to slow down, think. I passed an open door—the only open door I've seen since the day the old man passed away. I retrace my steps but can't find the door. I'm afraid it's been shut. I think it was purple. I start to run. Which one? Which one? I think I've missed a great opportunity. Then there it is, wide open and waiting. Beyond it I can see a table of food. Huge bowls of fruit. A platter of cakes. Freshly roasted meats. Simmering casseroles. Bread and butter and cheese. I rush through the door and race around the table. I taste a bit of all there is. I swallow huge handfuls of the things I like. I don't stop eating until my stomach hurts. Then I look back at the door. It's mirrored and shut. I'm in a large room with a floor-to-ceiling window. Next to the window's a chair. I sit in the chair and look out at the world. All I can see is

knees. I realize it hasn't a newspaper in front of it. Realize it hasn't a number on its face. ☐ I hold my head as high as I can. I dog-paddle

a huge mirror-covered building reflecting a mirror-covered building. I close my eyes and go to sleep.

When I wake, I'm thirsty. Everything in the room is dark blue. The table of food is gone. The window, opaque. The door is still shut. Its mirrored surface replaced with stone. To my right is a hall. I walk down it in search of something to drink. The further I go, the lighter it gets. It ends in a room similar to the one I left. Against the far wall is a bed. On either side of the bed is a hall. On the floor at the foot of the bed someone has used thick white chalk to draw the outline of a body. At its centre there's a dark stain. Beside it, a pile of paper clips. They're shiny and new and perfect. I crouch down and examine them. They're bigger than the ones I have in my pocket. I pick them up and they are mine—ninety-seven more paper clips to call my own.

I sense that I am being watched. I leap up and spin around, but am alone. I scan the room for surveillance cameras. I look under the bed. I don't find anything that can record my presence. I don't find anything to quench my thirst. There's now

more than I crawl. My eyes are level with the newspapers floating on the surface of the floor. There is barely enough light to see their

only one hallway beside the bed. It's yellow and well-lit, lined with doors. Each door has a handle and a bell beside it. Ignoring the bell, I grip the handle of the closest door. It's smooth and warm. I take a tight grip and twist my wrist. It silently turns and the door easily opens. Bright light shines through and music fills the air. It's light and lively, happy music. It seems to promise joy, but the light hurts my eyes and I have to look away. As my sight clears, I see a paper clip a few steps away. I close the door and pick it up. I step to another and pick it up as well. Then another and another. The trail of paper clips leads me down the hall. They're all different sizes. Some are old. Some are new. I stuff them in my pockets as fast as I can.

I come to another chalk outline of a body. This one is smaller and lies beside a broken bottle. There's a little liquid left in the bottom of the bottle. My thirst returns. I smell the liquid and burn my sinuses. I smell it again. It's not as bad as I thought. A quick taste might not hurt. The food was fine. I look down at the chalk outline. I lift the bottle to my lips. I take a deep

edges. I can just manage to read the print on the folds beneath the photographs: *Serene liberation and happiness; Liberating happiness*

breath and close my eyes. I throw the liquid down the hall. It hits the wall and drips to the floor. Small holes appear in the carpet and thin wisps of smoke drift my way.

I look down at the outline. Whoever he was, he's no longer in the game. He seems to have died without any paper clips. I vow to myself not to let that happen to me. I'm standing at a junction where several halls meet. They all look the same. Each one might lead to more paper clips. Each one might lead to something I can drink. I close my eyes and listen. I hear water splashing into a pool. I open my eyes. The sound stops. I look to my right. There's a paper clip on the floor so I pick it up. It's like the one my father gave me— very small, plastic and green. I feel redeemed. I close my eyes and say a prayer. Hearing water, I move toward it. It takes me back the way I came. I suspect this means a loss of paper clips. I open my eyes. I'm standing in the centre of the dead man's outline.

I close my eyes and move toward the sound of water. I finger the paper clips in my pockets. They feel fragile and few and

in serenity; Happiness serenely liberates. □ I reach the door at the end of the hallway. It's so dark I'm not sure it's still there. I'm

Philip Arima

sadly lacking. I know I need more to start feeling safe. As the sound of water grows louder, I count my paper clips as best I can. My mouth gets dry and my throat feels tight. When I finish counting, I'm sure I must have made a mistake. The total is disturbingly low. Frustrated, I open my eyes. I'm standing in a hall with flat black walls, ceiling and floor. The air is stale. In front of me is a door. At its centre is the small three-line design I saw before. I push and it opens. Inside I can see another huge window and cardboard cartons lining the walls. They're all neatly stacked to shoulder height. I feel an urge between my legs. My breath rate increases. I remember the music. I'm incredibly thirsty.

I step through the door. It closes behind me. I rush to a carton and lift its lid. It's filled with boxes the size of my head. On the top of each box is a picture of a paper clip. Under each picture is a six-digit number. I open a box and stare at more paper clips than I've ever imagined. Cupping my hands, I lift hundreds of paper clips to my face. They wash over my skin and fall to the floor. At the next

exhausted and confused. I'm treading the carpet as if it is water. I raise my hands above my head. I kick harder with my legs. I lunge

stack of cartons, I do the same. I race around the room opening the top carton of every stack. I'm giddy and happy and don't know what to do. I wish I had a pen and paper to calculate all I own. I go to the door. It will not open. I press my ear against its surface. I close my eyes. I hear a splash.

forward. My hands connect. My perspective changes. The door has a number and newspaper. ■

Phlip Arima

About the Author

Phlip Arima is an Eurasian male with thick hair and hazel eyes. Almost five feet, nine inches and a hundred and forty-something pounds, he's slender and smooth and well-defined. He's open-minded and adventurous, seeking deep experiences with like-minded individuals. He's clean and safe and generally sane. His area code is 416.